1 2 3 4 5 6 7 8 9 10
❖
First Edition

MAURICE SENDAK'S
LITTLE BEAR

Emily's Birthday

BY ELSE HOLMELUND MINARIK
ILLUSTRATED BY CHRIS HAHNER

HarperFestival®
A Division of HarperCollins*Publishers*

"Look at all the new buds on this tree,

Little Bear," said Emily.

They were sitting on a comfortable

branch in their favorite apple tree.

Emily's doll, Lucy, kept them company.

"Look at the baby flowers," said Emily.

"Soon they will bloom.

They grow up very fast."

"Yes," said Little Bear,

"and become apples!"

Little Bear looked at all of the new buds.
"If these buds weren't here yesterday, that
means that they were born today," he said.
"Today is their birthday!"

"You're right, Little Bear," said Emily.

"And do you know what tomorrow is?"

Little Bear said that he didn't.

"It's my birthday," said Emily.

"Oh, my!" said Little Bear.

"I had forgotten!"

"That's all right," said Emily.

"Will you still be able to come over

tomorrow?" asked Little Bear.

"Oh, yes," said Emily.

As Little Bear walked home that

afternoon, he thought of all the

things he had to do.

He was going to give Emily

a birthday party!

A party has to be with our friends.

I'll invite Hen and Duck and Owl and

Cat, thought Little Bear.

Mother Bear will be there—it's at our

house, after all.

Little Bear's head was full of ideas:

He would make a cake.

Mother Bear would make a nice lunch.

And Emily's friends would sing
"Happy Birthday."

It was time for supper.

As Little Bear sat at the table,

he told Mother Bear of his plans

for Emily's birthday.

"But it's too late to make a cake,

Little Bear," said Mother Bear.

Little Bear said, "Well, as long as our

friends are here, it will be a fine party!"

Little Bear hopped into bed.

Emily should have a fine party.

She is such a good friend!

He went to sleep with a smile on
his face.

When Little Bear woke up the next
morning, the sun was shining brightly.

He climbed out of bed.

He was excited.

It was Emily's birthday!

Little Bear had so much to do.

He called to Mother Bear,

"I am going out to invite all of our

friends to the party.

I'll be back soon."

On his walk, Little Bear's mind was
full of ideas for Emily.
It was going to be a wonderful party,
a wonderful party for a sweet friend.

Little Bear found Hen cleaning.

"Hen, it is Emily's birthday.

Will you come to her party?"

Hen said, "Oh, yes, Little Bear.

What time is the party?"

"I think noon is a good time for a
party," said Little Bear.
"Noon is a very good time for a
party," said Hen.

Little Bear found Cat,

and Cat liked the idea of a party.

He said, "We could give Emily a

birthday present."

"That's a good idea, Cat," said Little Bear.

"A birthday isn't a birthday without

a present."

Cat said he would try to think of something.

"I will see you at noon!" said Little Bear.

On the way to Owl's house,

Little Bear's stomach rumbled.

I'm hungry, he thought.

I wonder what time it is?

Little Bear found Owl and Duck.

"Oooh, a party!" said Duck.

"We will be pleased to come," said Owl.

"Then follow me," said Little Bear.

"It must be almost noon."

Little Bear, Owl, and Duck came upon Cat
and Hen on the path to Little Bear's house.
As they walked, they practiced singing
"Happy Birthday."

"That sounded good," said Little Bear.

As they neared Little Bear's house,

they came upon Emily's favorite

apple tree.

All the buds had now become flowers.

Little Bear said, "Let's take some
branches back to the house.

Emily will love these."

Duck, Cat, Hen, and Owl watched
for Emily while Little Bear set
the table.
Soon they saw her.
They all stood by the door,
just out of her sight.

When Emily knocked, Mother Bear opened

the door.

Little Bear, Hen, Duck, Cat, and Owl

jumped out and yelled, "Happy Birthday!"

Little Bear gave Emily a flowering branch.

Emily's friends sang "Happy
Birthday," and gave her a
basket of birthday cookies.
Later, she skipped home to her
family.

*I will have had two birthday
parties*, Emily thought.
Lucy loves that!